The BLUES Go Birding
Across America

WITHDRAWN

Meet the BLUES

BING
Band Leader
Favorite color: Maroon
Bing loves:
- singing songs
- rhyming words
- using maps

Favorite expression:
"Let's cruise, BLUES!"

LULU
Blue Belle
Favorite color: Pink
Lulu loves:
- dressing up
- making friends
- taking photos

Favorite expression:
"Think pink!"

UNO
One-of-a-Kind
Favorite color: Orange
Uno loves:
- playing the guitar
- loons and rubber duckies
- and not much else

Favorite expression:
"Uh-oh!"

EGGBERT
Super Birder
Favorite color: Green
Eggbert loves
- watching birds
- reading about birds
- talking about birds

Favorite expression:
"Birding is the best!"

SAMMI
Sportster
Favorite color: Yellow
Sammi loves
- doing ALL sports
- getting a good workout
- going on adventures

Favorite expression:
"Girl power!"

By Carol L. Malnor and Sandy F. Fuller ✳ Illustrated by Louise Schroeder
DAWN PUBLICATIONS

For bird lovers of all ages. — CLM

For W. Ellsworth, who always knew The BLUES would fly, with much love. — SFF

For my daughters, Suzanne, Camille and Sophie and my husband, Joseph. — LS

ACKNOWLEDGEMENTS

The authors especially wish to thank Glenn Hovemann and Muffy Weaver for helping the BLUES take flight. They spent countless hours with us envisioning the characters and writing and revising the manuscript. Their energy and creativity is evident on every page. We consider them our "co-authors" as well as our skilled editors, publishers, and friends.

Many thanks to the teachers, parents, and children who provided valuable feedback and suggestions during the creation of the manuscript: Andrea Yocum and her first grade students of the class of 2008-2009 at Yuba Environmental Science Charter Academy in Oregon House, California; Usha Dermond; Paul Green; Karen Bush; Ron, Kathleen, and Louisa Malnor; and Katelyn Beaver. Grateful appreciation goes to Barbara Herkert for the use of her beautiful United States map. Thanks also to Anne James-Rosenberg of the Cornell Lab and ornithologist Edward C. (Ted) Beedy for their generous assistance in assuring accuracy about birds.

Important sources for bird information include *All About Birds* (Cornell Lab of Ornithology: www.allaboutbirds.org) and *The Birds of North America Online* (Cornell Lab of Ornithology and the American Ornithologists' Union: http://bna.birds.cornell.edu).

A Sharing Nature With Children Book

Library of Congress Cataloging-in-Publication Data

Malnor, Carol.

  The Blues go birding across America / by Carol L. Malnor and Sandy F. Fuller ; illustrated by Louise Schroeder. -- 1st ed.

      p. cm.

  "A sharing nature With children book"--Verso t.p.

  Summary: Looking for a new song to sing, five little birds go on a birdwatching trip and see species from the bald eagle in Alaska to mallards in Boston.

  ISBN 978-1-58469-124-2 (hardcover) -- ISBN 978-1-58469-125-9 (pbk.) [1. Birds--Fiction. 2. Bird watching--Fiction.] I. Fuller, Sandy Ferguson. II. Schroeder, Louise, ill. III. Title.

  PZ7.M29635Bl 2010

  [Fic]--dc22

                    2009036163

Manufactured by Regent Publishing Services, Hong Kong,
Printed January, 2010, in ShenZhen, Guangdong, China

10 9 8 7 6 5 4 3 2 1
First Edition

Book design and computer producton by Patty Arnold, *Menagerie Design and Publishing*

DAWN PUBLICATIONS

12402 Bitney Springs Road
Nevada City, CA 95959
530-274-7775
nature@dawnpub.com

We're the BLUES! We're a band of birds who like to sing. Uno plays the guitar. Bing is our band leader, and got us our first live concert. There was sure to be a big crowd!

But we had a problem. We needed a new song to sing. Here's what happened.

We were in our Clubhouse when Bing got an idea for a trip. "It's spring!" he said. "Birds are singing all across America. Let's tour the country and listen for some great new sounds before our big show." Bing began to map our route as he sang *"from sea to shining sea."*

Eggbert grabbed his birding field guide. As we gathered up our gear, Uno sat on his bed with his guitar and mumbled, "I'll only go along if we hear my favorite bird—an amazing laughing loon."

"Hmm," said Bing. He looked over his list, but didn't say a word.

We woke up at dawn's early light. Bing shouted, "Ready? Set! LIFTOFF!" We flew along Alaska's rugged coast in search of the U.S. National Bird—the Bald Eagle. "What a great way to begin our trip across America!" sang Sammi.

Soon Eggbert spotted an eagle on a huge nest, so we landed on a nearby cliff and dropped in for a closer look. "What an awesome bird," whispered Bing. But then we heard *kak-kak-kak*. "That's not musical," he said, disappointed. "We're out of here."

Sammi's Notebook

This is the first page in my bird watching journal. It's yellow, like my hat.

Ben Franklin wanted the Wild Turkey to be the symbol for the U.S., but I'm glad it's the Bald Eagle. Forty years ago they almost became extinct. Now they're protected by a law, and they're making a strong comeback. Go, Eagles!

FIELD GUIDE

BALD EAGLE

Body Size: 28-38 in.

Wingspan: 80 in.

Habitat: Forests along seacoasts, large rivers, and lakes.

Food: Carrion, fish; sometimes small birds and animals.

Sound: *kleek-kik-ik-ik-ik* or *kak-kak-kak.*

Uh-oh!!

Cowabunga! Girls rule!

Then we flew over miles of ocean until we finally dropped into the warm waters of Hawaii. As we rode the waves, a huge Black-footed Albatross glided by. "He can soar for months without touching the ground!" Eggbert said.

"Doesn't he ever get thirsty?" sang Sammi. "I am."

"He scoops up salt water as he flies," Eggbert explained. "Hey, Uno, only two other birds can drink salt water—and one of them is the loon."

"But this guy doesn't sing!" Bing exclaimed. "No time to relax, BLUES. Aloha, Albatross."

Lulu's Notebook

We were lucky to see a Black-footed Albatross. They spend most of their time flying far out to sea. Once a young albatross leaves its nest, it flies over the ocean for several years (some scientists think as many as ten years) before returning to land. That's endurance!

I thought the albatross was wearing a bracelet. But Eggbert told me it's called a band. Scientists put bands on them so they can track them wherever they go. I'd like to wear a pretty band, too! I'm glad Eggbert is here. He knows so much cool stuff about birds!

The albatross has a bracelet! I want one!

Lulu, that's a band, not a bracelet!

FIELD GUIDE

BLACK-FOOTED ALBATROSS

Body Size: 25-29 in.

Wingspan: 76-85 in.

Habitat: Pacific Ocean; nests on Hawaiian Islands.

Food: Eggs of flying fish; also squid, adult flying fish, and other fish.

Sound: Usually silent when alone. Calls include *haw-haw* and *eh*.

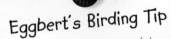

Sammi's Notebook

Even though it was foggy, it was easy for me to find Ring-billed Gulls. They are the most common gull in the U.S.

They eat just about anything. But not everything they eat is good for them. Sometimes they eat bread that people give to them. Then the bread swells up in their tummies and makes them really sick. Their natural food is fish. Eating fish keeps them healthy.

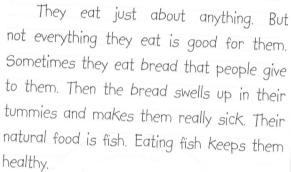

FIELD GUIDE

RING-BILLED GULL

Body Size: 17-21 in.

Wingspan: 41-46 in.

Habitat: Ocean bays and beaches, inland lakes, plowed fields, and cities.

Food: Insects, earthworms, rodents, grain, fish, garbage.

Sound: Loud *kakakakakaka*; shrill *oooww*; series of *a-a-a-a-a-a*.

We flew across the Pacific, under the Golden Gate Bridge and swooped onto a fishing boat in San Francisco Bay. "I'm wet, cold, and hungry," grumbled Uno.

Ring-billed Gulls were everywhere, screeching. "We could follow them," Eggbert yelled over the noise. "They know where to get fast food."

"Gulls sure can be loud," shouted Bing, "but they don't have harmony—no new song for us here. Let's fly high to someplace dry."

Eggbert's Notebook

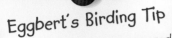

This bird is really interesting! Here's what my field guide says about the Greater Roadrunner:

- They are able to fly, but they have short wings and prefer to run along the ground.
- Using their long legs, they can run up to 15 miles an hour. They are the fastest running bird that also flies. (The ostrich is the fastest running bird, but it doesn't fly.)
- They're quick enough to catch a rattlesnake.

FIELD GUIDE

GREATER ROADRUNNER

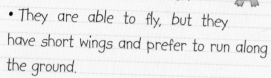

Body Size: 20-21 in.
Wingspan: 19 in.
Habitat: Open, dry scrubland.
Food: Variety of insects, spiders, snakes, scorpions, lizards, small birds, and rodents.
Sound: Call is a *co-coo-coo-coo-cooooo*, also *putt-putt-putt-whirrr*.

On our way to the Southwest, we dipped low over the Grand Canyon. "Steep and deep beneath!" chirped Bing, who loves words that rhyme. After stopping at a banding station we touched down in New Mexico. Admiring our new bands, we were nearly run over by a Greater Roadrunner chasing breakfast—if you can call a scorpion breakfast.

Putt-putt-putt-whirrr!

"He should say BEEP BEEP!" sang Sammi.

"Interesting sound effects," said Bing. "The roadrunner sure is fast, but it doesn't have a song for us. Let's hit the road!"

I'm Uno, the banded Birdito!

Bing's Notebook

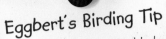

Most birds are active very early in the morning and late in the afternoon. Owls are different. They are nocturnal—active at night. That's when they hunt. They can surprise their prey—the animals they eat—because they fly so quietly.

They swallow their food whole. Then they cough up a pellet of the parts they can't digest, like the fur, teeth, and bones. Eggbert found lots of owl pellets under the tree where the owl roosted.

FIELD GUIDE

GREAT HORNED OWL

Body Size: 18-25 in.
Wingspan: 40-57 in.
Habitat: Woodlands, farms, forests, deserts, towns, and cities.
Food: Small mammals, small owls and other birds, amphibians, reptiles.
Sound: Deep hooting call *hoo-h'HOO--hoo-hoo.*

Rock-a-bye OW-LL, in the tree top.

Some more s'mores, anyone?

We flew high over the craggy peaks of the Continental Divide, arriving late at Rocky Mountain National Park. Pitching camp by flashlight was so-o-o spooky!

"SHHH! Listen!" whispered Lulu. "WHO-WHO is that?"

Bing knew just by the sound. "Lulu, it's a Great Horned Owl."

"Horns!" she screamed.

"Relax, those are just feathers," Eggbert reassured her.

"Ghostly songs won't work for us," declared Bing. "Let's bag it for tonight BLUES! Sleeping bags, that is!"

Next we landed on a sea of grass—the Great Plains. "*O beautiful, for spacious skies*," Bing crooned, "*for amber waves of grain!*"

"What a great melody!" exclaimed Sammi. Bing beamed. "Sorry, Bing," Sammi said, pointing to the bird on the fencepost, "not you—that guy."

Eggbert told us it was a Western Meadowlark, famous for its beautiful voice.

"We could try his song at our concert," said Bing, "but it would be tricky to learn so many fancy whistles. Let's keep looking. We'll soon be famous, too!"

Wow! It's the Nebraska State Bird!

But I thought we were in Kansas.

Eggbert's Birding Tip

Look for a bird's special colors and markings. They are called "field marks."

Uno's Notebook

We finally heard a bird that could carry a tune. The Western Meadowlark's song was terrific! He sang so many different notes and trills! Really cool!

Lulu liked how he looked with a big, black "V" on his bright yellow chest. I guess fancy songs and flashy feathers always impress females.

It's the Kansas State Bird, too.

AH-CHOOO! Hay fever.

FIELD GUIDE

WESTERN MEADOWLARK

Body Size: 6-10 in.

Wingspan: 16 in.

Habitat: Open country, grasslands, pastures, fields, and roadsides.

Food: Insects, grain, and weed seeds.

Sound: Song is series of melodious whistles, like a flute. Call is a sharp *chupp*.

Bald is cute.

We followed the Central Flyway deep into the heart of Texas and *smelled* our way to the next bird on our list, a vulture—the Turkey Vulture, to be exact.

Eggbert, who loves ALL birds, had something good to say about him. "He's a helpful citizen who keeps our environment clean by eating dead animals. Messy job, but someone has to do it."

"I don't know how vultures stand the smell," squeaked Lulu through her clothespin.

"No music here, and time is running out!" said Bing. "Let's wing it."

Eggbert's Birding Tip

By watching carefully you'll discover why birds behave as they do.

Lulu's Notebook

This bird got its name because its bald head looks like a turkey's head. At first I thought it was UGLY—but then I completely changed my mind!

Plus, I found out that there's a good reason vultures don't have any feathers on their heads. They eat dead animals—carrion. If vultures had feathers on their heads, they would get really dirty when they ate.

Even though vultures aren't pretty to look at when they're on the ground, they look sooo graceful circling high in the air.

FIELD GUIDE

TURKEY VULTURE

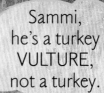

Body Size: 25-32 in.

Wingspan: 67-70 in.

Habitat: Rangeland, farmland, and forest. Roosts in large trees.

Food: Dead animals (carrion).

Sound: Mostly silent. Sometimes makes a hiss or a grunt.

Eggbert's Birding Tip

Listen! You can find and identify birds by sound.

Eggbert's Notebook

The Pileated (PILL-ee-a-ted or PI-lee-at-ed) Woodpecker doesn't drum to make music. It drums to warn other woodpeckers to stay out of his part of the forest.

I got a good look at the woodpecker's tongue. It extended 6 inches to spear his food. His tongue is so long it wraps around his skull inside of his head.

He doesn't get a headache because special tissue inside his head acts like a shock absorber. Also, his brain fits snugly inside his skull.

FIELD GUIDE

PILEATED WOODPECKER

Body Size: 16-19 in.

Wingspan: 26-30 in.

Habitat: Forests with large trees.

Food: Carpenter ants, beetle larvae, insects, fruits, and nuts.

Sound: Call a loud, ringing *kuk-kuk-kuk.* "Song" is a loud rhythmic drumming sound made by pecking on trees or telephone poles.

He's stabbing beetles!

We crossed the mighty Mississippi River on our long flight to the north woods of Michigan. "*Over the river and through the woods,*" Bing sang.

A loud *rap-rap-rap* echoed through the pines. We found a Pileated Woodpecker stabbing beetles and ants.

Uno squealed, "Nice sound! LET'S JAM!" and picked up his guitar.

We played until Bing reminded us, "We don't need a drummer, but we do need a new melody. Let's beat it."

Sammi's Notebook

The backyard feeder attracted birds so we could see them up close. Songbirds like the goldfinch learn their songs from adult birds, sort of like human babies learning to talk by listening to their parents. It can take several months for songbirds to learn their songs perfectly.

Eggbert identified and counted all the birds. The brightly colored males were especially easy to identify. He'll send his count to Project FeederWatch at the Cornell Lab, where it will be used by scientists. I'm going to be like Eggbert and count birds, too!

FIELD GUIDE

FEEDER BIRDS

American Goldfinch
Song: *per-chic-o-ree* and *sei silieee*.

Northern Cardinal
Song: *Cheer, cheer, cheer, what, what, what, what.* Also *pretty, pretty, pretty.*

Ruby-throated Hummingbird
Sound: Rapid, squeaky chipping. Humming sound from wings.

After passing over the vast Great Lakes and into Ohio, we spotted a backyard feast. "Goody! Time for a picnic," sang Sammi.

While we grabbed some tasty treats, Eggbert grabbed his FeederWatch list. "This place is perfect!" he said, as he counted American Goldfinches, Northern Cardinals, and Ruby-throated Hummingbirds.

Per-CHIC-o-ree! Ta-DEE-di-di! Sei-silleeee?

"Great neighborhood," chirped Lulu. "These songbirds are so musical!"

"Cool tunes," agreed Bing. "Let's remember these melodies. But for now, eat up BLUES. It's time to cruise!"

Good food always draws a crowd.

As we landed at a grand old Southern estate, Lulu chirped, "Wow! Listen to all the different birds singing!"

""That's just one bird, a Northern Mockingbird," Eggbert explained. "He imitates other birds. And he will sing for hours at night, especially when the moon is full. That's why some people call him a NIGHTingale. Get it?"

Lulu giggled. "Eggbert, you told a joke—almost!"

"Yeah, aren't I a crack-up?" Eggbert grinned.

"Whatever he's called, let's not copy a copycat," said Bing. "C'mon, time to go!"

Fireflies are also called lightning bugs.

Eggbert's Birding Tip

It's fun just to watch birds. You don't have to identify them by name.

Uno's Notebook

Northern Mockingbirds are real singers! They sing during the day and at night, too! They learn songs from other birds and then use them to create their own. They even copy manmade sounds like cell phones.

Both males and females sing, repeating their songs over and over. And like all good musicians, they continue to learn new songs throughout their life. Some mockingbirds know over 200 songs. That's more than the BLUES!

That bird can sing anything!

But can he sing a loony tune?

Is a copycat like a real cat?

FIELD GUIDE

NORTHERN MOCKINGBIRD

Body Size: 8-10 in.
Wingspan: 12-14 in.
Habitat: Open ground with shrubby vegetation, parks, farms, and suburbs.
Food: Fruits and insects.
Sound: Copies the songs and calls of other birds.

We flew by moonlight over Florida's Okefenokee Swamp to the Gulf of Mexico. At sunrise, we tiptoed past a Roseate Spoonbill.

"Great beak. Perfect for spooning up breakfast," sang Sammi.

"Look, it just swallows everything whole—fish, slugs, bugs, and all!" gulped Lulu. "It'll probably get a stomachache."

"Well, step it up before he barfs," joked Bing. "Ready on the wing!"

Uh-oh!

Finally I'm tall enough to play basketball.

Lulu, do YOU only come in pink?

Oooh, do they only come in pink?

Lulu's Notebook

Roseate Spoonbills are my favorite color—pink! Sometimes they're confused with flamingos. Both are pink wading birds with long legs. But their beaks are totally different.

I learned that I don't have to worry about the spoonbill getting a stomachache. Swallowing food whole is natural for him.

People used to kill spoonbills for their feathers, which were put on ladies' hats. Then wildlife refuges were created to protect them. Lots of spoonbills live in the Ding Darling Wildlife Refuge in Florida.

FIELD GUIDE

ROSEATE SPOONBILL

Body Size: 28-34 in.

Wingspan: 47-51 in.

Habitat: Very shallow warm salt or fresh water.

Food: Small fish, tiny shell fish, slugs, water insects, shrimp.

Sound: Low grunting sounds.

We followed the warm Gulf Stream north to Boston to visit some famous urban birds on the Charles River. A Mallard mom was taking her ducklings for their first swim.

"Not too close," Eggbert reminded us. "Make way for ducklings!"

It was almost time for our show on the White House lawn, and we still didn't have a new song to sing. Where were we going to find one?

But as usual, Bing kept us moving. "Quack, let's row. I mean, quick, let's go!"

Sammi's Notebook

The Mallard ducklings could swim even though they hatched only yesterday. The air in their feathers keeps them on top of the water.

Mother Mallard was very protective. She was mostly brown, so she and the babies could easily hide, or be camouflaged, when on land. But Father Mallard had a bright green head. He doesn't take care of babies, so he doesn't need to be camouflaged.

Quack!

Quack!

Quack!

CRRRAAAK!

FIELD GUIDE

MALLARD DUCK

Body Size: 20-26 in.

Wingspan: 32-37 in.

Habitat: All wetlands, ponds, lakes, rivers; also parks and fields.

Food: Seeds and roots of water plants, insects, snails, tadpoles, frogs, earthworms, small fish, grain.

Sound: Female gives loud series of quacks. Male makes softer *rab*, *yeeb*, or *kwek*.

It was the Fourth of July. "Happy Birthday USA," sang Sammi. We arrived on the White House lawn to find a crowd of American Robins.

"What a great audience! I bet they've been waiting for us since dawn," said Bing. "Good thing they've had plenty to munch on!"

But we still weren't ready for the show! What song would Bing choose? Then he passed out our song sheets. To our surprise, it was an old favorite! "Time to sing!" he said. "All together now."

And the BLUES sang as we never had before.

FROM . . . SEA . . . TO . . .
SHINING . . . SEA!

Bing's Notebook

The robin is sometimes called "America's favorite songbird." It was the perfect bird to have at our concert.

The robin's song, "cheer up, cheer up," reminded us to be cheerful and happy. Listening to it, I realized that all the birds we heard on our trip across America had taught us something special.

FIELD GUIDE

AMERICAN ROBIN

Body Size: 8-11 in.

Wingspan: 12-16 in.

Habitat: Forests, woodlands, and gardens, short grass, shrubs, trees, cities, and suburbs.

Food: Earthworms and fruit.

Sound: Song a musical whistled cheerily, *cheer up, cheer up, cheerily, cheer up.* Call note a sharp *chup*.

"SPLASHDOWN!" sang Sammi.

"America IS beautiful. And SO BIG. But there's no place like home."

"The BLUES are the best!" chirped Lulu. "We sounded AMAZING!"

"Birding is the best, too!" added Eggbert. "Every bird we saw on our trip was unique and inspired our singing in some special way."

"You're right," agreed Bing as he looked over his list. "We outdid ourselves. Just like the meadowlark, we really gave it feeling! And big energy, like the roadrunner. And good cheer, like the robins. And so much more! We didn't need a new song after all."

"But I didn't hear a loon," grumbled Uno.

"Not to worry, Uno," said Bing. "We'll take lots more trips!"

Eggbert's Birding Tip
Look for new birds to add to your list whenever you take a trip.

Bing's Checklist

- ☐ Bald Eagle—**Be strong.**
- ☐ Black-footed Albatross—**Keep going.**
- ☐ Ring-billed Gull—**Stay healthy.**
- ☐ Greater Roadrunner—**Have energy.**
- ☐ Great Horned Owl—**Pay attention.**
- ☐ Western Meadowlark—**Express yourself.**
- ☐ Turkey Vulture—**Help others.**
- ☐ Pileated Woodpecker—**Stay focused.**
- ☐ Backyard Feeder Birds—**Listen carefully.**
- ☐ Northern Mockingbird—**Learn from others.**
- ☐ Roseate Spoonbill—**Protect nature.**
- ☐ Mallard—**Care for family.**
- ☐ American Robin—**Be cheerful.**

FIELD GUIDE

RESOURCES

Peterson Guide to Birds of North America or *Peterson First Guide to Birds* by Roger Tory Peterson.

Birds, A Golden Guide from St. Martin's Press.

The Young Birder's Guide to Birds of Eastern North America by Bill Thompson III and Julie Zickefoose.

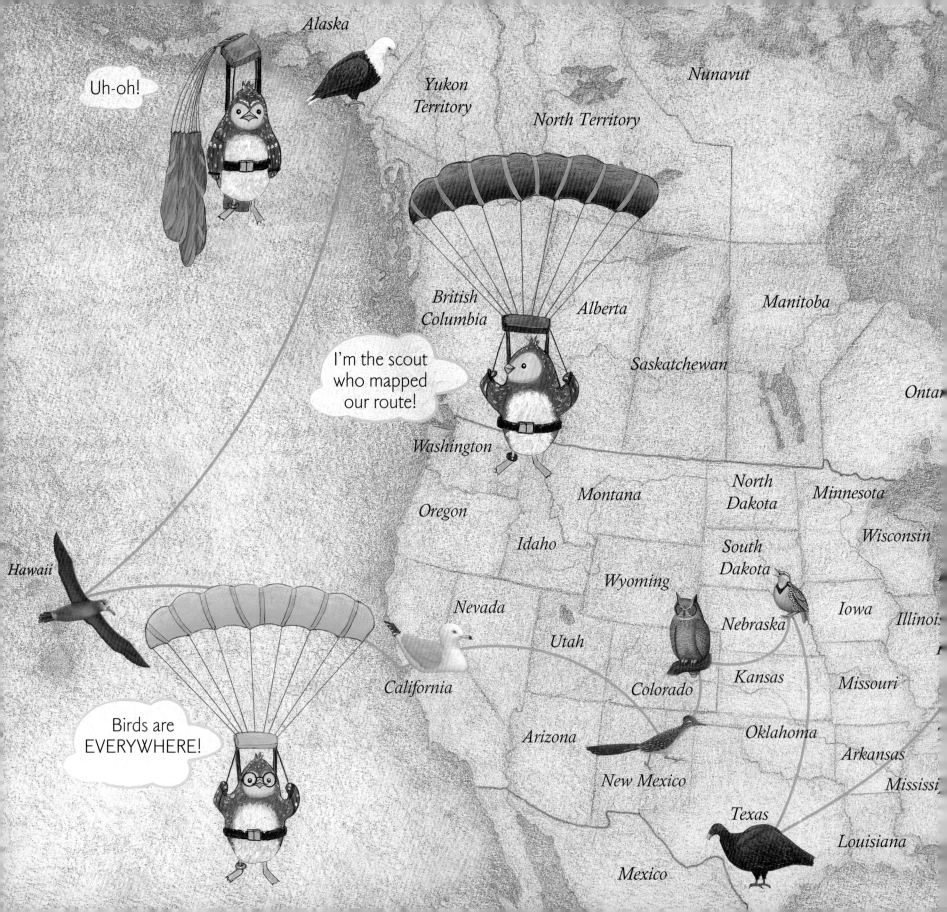

Greenland

Newfoundland

Quebec

New
Brunswick — Prince Edward Island

Nova Scotia

Maine

Vermont
— New Hampshire
— Massachusetts
New York
— Rhode Island
Pennsylvania
— Connecticut
— New Jersey
Ohio — Maryland
West — Delaware
Virginia Virginia

North
Carolina

South
Carolina

rgia

Florida

Let's hit
the beach!

Let's go
sailing next!

Bing's Notebook

We traveled all across America to find birds. Some of them were in national parks (NP) and others were in national wildlife refuges (NWR). We marked the places where we saw them on our map. But most of these birds are really common and can be seen in lots of other places—from sea to shining sea.

Where We Saw the Birds

Bald Eagle—Anchorage, AK
Black-footed Albatross—HI
Ring-billed Gull—San Francisco, CA
Greater Roadrunner—Chihuahuan Desert, NM
Great Horned Owl—Rocky Mountain NP, CO
Western Meadowlark—Ft. Niobrara NWR, NE
Turkey Vulture—Balcones Canyonlands NWR, TX
Pileated Woodpecker—Marquette, MI
Feeder Birds—Columbus, OH
Northern Mockingbird—Piedmont NWR, GA
Roseate Spoonbill—Ding Darling NWR, FL
Mallard—Boston, MA
American Robin—Washington, D. C.

How to Have More Fun with Birds

Three great bird-counting activities (www.birdsource.org):

- **The Christmas Bird Count**, first sponsored by the Audubon Society over 100 years ago, has become a winter tradition for many families.

- **The Great Backyard Bird Count** is an annual event sponsored by Audubon, the Cornell Lab, and Wild Birds Unlimited. Bird watchers of all ages and levels of experience participate.

- **Project FeederWatch** is a winter-long survey of birds that visit feeders. Anyone with an interest in birds can participate. Scientists at Cornell Lab use the results.

How to Learn More about Birds

Cornell Lab of Ornithology—Provides wonderful resources for kids and families and excellent curriculum, projects, and materials for teachers. www.birds.cornell.edu All About Birds is the lab's online guide to birds and bird watching. www.allaboutbirds.org

National Audubon Society—Local chapters around the country sponsor bird walks, nature outings, educational programs, and special events. Many great resources are available online. www.audubon.org

American Birding Association—Programs for young birders including camps, scholarships, contests, and newsletters. www.aba.org

The Birdwatcher's Digest—A magazine filled with how-to tips, bird identification, gardening for birds, and more. www.birdwatchersdigest.com.

About the Bird-Lovers Who Wrote and Illustrated This Book

CAROL L. MALNOR
Nature Book Lady

Favorite color: All shades of blue

Carol loves
- going birding
- writing books
- doing Tai Chi

Favorite expression:
"Mistakes are wonderful opportunities to learn."

Carol lives with her husband in the foothills of the Sierra Nevada, where she has breakfast with her backyard birds each morning.

SANDY F. FULLER
Kid-at-Heart

Favorite color: Blue (It's true!)

Sandy loves
- family and friends
- mountains and Maine
- guitars and gourmet

Favorite expression:
"FAR OUT!"

Sandy lives in Colorado, sharing mountain life with Riva (golden retriever), Ellsworth (aka Bill) and Scott and Kimberly (when they visit Mom!).

LOUISE SCHROEDER
World Traveler

Favorite color: Aquamarine

Louise loves
- being with family
- enjoying nature
- painting

Favorite expression:
"Let's go somewhere."

A native of rural Canada and visual creator of the Blues, Louise lives with her husband and three daughters in Las Vegas, Nevada.

THE BLUES invite parents, teachers, and kids to visit them at **www.thebluesgobirding.com**. You'll discover great birding resources, lesson plans, backyard bird watching tips, citizen science projects, coloring pages, and more.

Dawn Publications is dedicated to inspiring in children a deeper understanding and appreciation for all life on Earth. You can browse through our titles, download resources for teachers, and order at www.dawnpub.com, or call 800-545-7475.